I0692562

Anonymous

Party lights

The monkey congress

Anonymous

Party lights
The monkey congress

ISBN/EAN: 9783337235253

Printed in Europe, USA, Canada, Australia, Japan

Cover: Foto ©Andreas Hilbeck / pixelio.de

More available books at **www.hansebooks.com**

PARTY LIGHTS;

OR,

The Monkey Congress.

CHARACTERS:

STEVENS, ASHLEY ("impeacher Jeems"), BUTLER (the "Great American Spoon"), BEECHER (High-Winded"), BOUTWELL, SUMNER, WILSON, BOYNTON, COLFAX, LOGAN, COVODE ("Dirty Jack"), NYE (the "Western Slasher"), HORACE GREELEY, etc., etc., etc.

INSCRIBED TO MARK M. POMEROY ("Brick.")

WILLIAM D. McGREGOR, PUBLISHER,

HUDSON CITY, NEW JERSEY.

1869.

INTRODUCTION.

SATIRE has been considered in all ages one of the most effective weapons against the vices of the day. It has been the only whip under which the vicious and blatant demagogue could be made to surrender. "Men shrink from ridicule, when not from law," is a truth which has been verified in every age from the days of SALLUST to those of CHURCHILL, POPE and BYRON. It has been considered, among enlightened nations, a crime against the public weal to withhold censure where censure was due; and the writer who could the more forcibly expose the transgressor, and bring him into general contempt and ridicule, was awarded higher honor than statesman or divine. Hence it is, at this critical period of our country's history, we have endeavored to place in their true light some of the principal demagogues and howling fanatics who are endeavoring to destroy, for selfish ends, the equilibrium of our Government, and to nullify the genius of our institutions. We are sure no reader, of well-balanced mind, will say we have been more than justly censorious, when he reflects upon the acts of the National Congress during the past three years. There has been no arbitrary law too wicked to undertake. There has been no palpable villainy too monstrous to adopt. Three-fourths of the national domain, extending from the Mississippi to the Rocky Mountains, has been given away to subsidized corporations and monopolies. The painted bawd and moneyed lobbyist are, in truth, the country's lawmakers.

While there is ever present on the floors of Congress the man of capital, with scrip in his pocket for so many shares in a projected railroad, or an eligible spot on its line, to be given for a Congress-man's vote, there are scores of punks waiting in the ante-rooms, or handing in their scented cards to members on the floor. The most barefaced, the most outrageous and the most rascally fraud ever com-mitted upon an intelligent people has been this system of bargaining off the people's territory to the monopolist, who, true to the spirit of weak human nature, becomes, in time, a wealthy aristocrat, and an oppressor of the working classes. Hundreds of millions of acres have been disposed of in this way. Then again, Congress, to keep itself in power, has degraded—nay, made the elective franchise a farce in ten of the Southern States. It conferred the right of citizen-ship on a barbarous, ignorant race, who no more understand its principles than do droves of chattering monkeys. And this is the Congress which has the brazen impudence to raise a hue and cry about election frauds! This is the Congress which has the audacity to send a commission to make out a case in their favor, in the City of New York, by suborning English thieves and burglars, and bribing till-tappers! Did they send any commission to New York when they turned JAMES BROOKS out of his seat and gave it to WILLIAM E. DODGE? Everybody knows how they dealt with Senator STOCKTON of New Jersey. Our patience becomes exhausted as we dwell upon this subject. We warn the people that the party in power are unscru-pulous money-grabbers, who but yesterday, as it were, followed the vocation of peanut-venders, tin-peddlers, peons, and shysters.

It has, therefore, been our object in writing this work, to hold up to merited contempt some of the principal actors in our national drama, and awaken the eyes of a too confiding and forgiving people to the dangers which environ them.

I.

Since Vice has come so much of late in vogue,
Since people smile on every knavish rogue,
Since fools will louder laugh when true men sigh,
And more esteem to cheat and villify,
To lie and slander, scoff at all that's good,
And look with favor on the low and rude ;
Since mouthing rascals prate and bigots swear,
Justice, decried, implores me not to spare.
Lead on, then, Vice! I'll follow in thy track ;
I'll hold my nose, but never turn my back.
Have at you all—pariahs, hinds and pimps,
Vienna heroes* and close-bottled imps.

II.

Shoddy, all hail!   Enchanter of our race!
Raiser of scullions from their obscure place!
Let brilliant diamonds and the costly bead

The redoubtable Robert C. Schenck (dubbed "General"), M. C.
from Ohio, made Vienna memorable by his rapid flight from there
during the rebellion.   He scampered off on hearing the first gun of
the enemy.

Those heads adorn which never learnt to read.
Let bracelets fine those ruddy shoulders rub,
And clasps bedeck the mistress of the tub.
Let golden belts incase the lusty zones
Of those whose husbands live by boiling bones.
Trot out, O Fashion, all your painted hags,
Let dirty dabchicks flutter in silken rags ;
Let brainless fops the human race degrade,
And pass their days not knowing why they're made.

III.

Hell was illum'd and gave a joyous route ;
Old devils quaff'd and threw their wine about ;
And winks went round, with gibe, and laugh and leer—
(Knowledge satanic of the coming cheer) ;
The furnace echoed with each jolly shout ;
And gluttons danced, though long confined with gout ;
As old Nick's post, a black and fleet-wing'd sprite,
Arrived with news which made their hearts delight.
    " 'Tis true," quoth he ; "believe me, on this day
The Pilgrim bigots reach'd the penal bay."*
    High on his throne, in grand and regal state,
The awful Devil press'd his royal weight.
Around the court the courtiers gravely plod ;
Business looked dull and Nick began to nod ;
While flames of red and blue his forehead fann'd,

* Massachusetts Bay.

Morpheus enrob'd him with a gentle hand.
His mouth lay open, and his great tongue hung out,
'Pon which a hundred elves soon skipp'd about.
His massive head was one extensive hall,
Where each young devil had a separate stall.
All grades of rogues were represented here,
From old Jack Covode down to pirate Weir.
These toiling elves, whene'er their master snores,
Trip lightly down his mouth and out of doors.

   In barb'd array, and in repellant mood,
Atop his ears two watchful sentries stood;
Astride his sconce, prepared to sound alarm,
A duce displayed a trumpet on his arm.
One long shrill blast from this metallic horn
His Highness wakes and all his subjects warn;
And as he shakes himself from his repose,
The elves that miss his mouth, shoot up his nose.

IV.

" What dire misfortune now befalls the great?
Advance, my post. What news heard you of late?"
   Thus spake the King infernal, raising high
His tail furcated, pressed by either thigh.
   The postboy thus: " This day, most mighty sire,
(If I speak false, then on me fall your ire),
A dolorous herd,—alas! to Neptune's shame—
Reached Plymouth rock, and Pilgrims is their name."
   As faith and doubt each motion would supply,
Reflection strained itself in Satan's eye;

And doubting thus, he touch'd the postboy's wing,
Aud said in Holland still the bigots sing;
And gravely questioned of their new abode,
As Neptune's self despised the filthy load.

  Annoyed at this, the sprite indignant grew,
Piled oath on oath, and swore 'twas most true.
" By hell," he cries, " and by its damning laws,
The Pilgrims claim the Indians' lands and squaws.
They moan and pray : the rocks with anthems peal ;
And Heaven's invoked to sanction what they steal."

  " These points are rather taking, I confess ;
But as I never set my plans on guess,
Return to Plymouth, close survey the crew ;
If they are Puritans, their hides are blue."

  Thus said his Highness, and away the sprite,
Cleaving the dark realms of eternal night,
Straining, craning, through thunderbolts and hail,
With flame-eyed dragons pressing on his tail,
So swift of wing that, ere the morning cock,
He dropp'd his pinions high on Plymouth rock.
A moment's pause, and then with subtle care,
He spread his wings and shot again through air.
But all was still as death ; in vain his hunt ;
Nothing was heard, except the cough or grunt
Of a redskin. The night was pitchy dark,
And naught to be seen, save a dragon's spark.
At length, with morn, awoke the whining pack,
When sprite and dragons viewed them front and back.
But truss'd so close in gurrah, plaids and hose,
The only proof of blueness was their nose.

V.

High in a tree, concealed from public gaze,
The elf attunes his pipe and sweetly plays.
Soon on the sward the lusty Debs appear,
And clownish Ebs, with large splay feet draw near.
The ring is formed; the dancers beat the ground,
While vigorous music make the rustics bound.
Round and round, with barbarous flings and jigs,
The Debs shake their leaves, and the Ebs their figs;
Long, scrawny arms encircle pliant zones,
And fustian yieldeth to protruding bones.
On, on they danced, till all the fustian fell,
When sprite and dragons bent their flight to hell.

VI.

"All hail, my post!" his sable Highness cries—
"Out, my fond hopes! I read them in your eyes;
Or speed you back to say my hopes are vain?
Have those fell bigots crossed the Western main?"
"Good news, my liege, o'er buoys thy servant's wing,
And you'll rejoice, I'm sure, at what I bring.
At thy command, the whining pack I found;
I scann'd them closely and surveyed them round;
But small details I shall not now pursue;
Suffice it, sire, that all their hides are blue."
Satan looked wise, and calmly weighed the case,
And moved his tail with thoughtful, gentle grace;

When soon a plan of wondrous strange device
(A plan, perhaps, more delicate than nice)
Flashed on his mind; and then, with grave import,
He raised his head, and said to all his court:
"The windy pilgrim that may this way wend
His doleful shade, and all pure air offend,
No more I'll roast, but with the bean-fed Jake
Bellows, no fuel, for the furnace make."
Sad disappointment fell on those around;
Some curs'd and swore, some stamp'd and kicked the
    ground.
They nursed their patience for a glorious roast,
Damn'd by the recent order of their host.

I'll now to Congress, with my burnished pen,
And show how monkeys ape the ways of men.

VII.

'Tis mooncalf ASHLEY riots on the floor,
Blest with the smiles of you admiring wh—e.
He ramps, he stamps, he turns him front and back,
The doxy's apis and her Pudding Jack;
As jockeys pat the steed that he may win,
The barber smoothed his hair and shaved his chin.
Wild to get loose, with self-approvance drunk,
Now 'tis "Mr. Speaker," now "Mistress Punk."*

* James M. Ashley, better known as Impeacher Ashley, has fre-
quently been called to order in the House of Representatives for ad-
dressing flash punks in the gallery, instead of the Speaker. He flatters
himself on being what is called among pumpkin heads a "lady-killer."

His soul is bent on high immortal fame,
Since Momus last with JOHNSON spread his name.*
See that design! Lo! how the boot-blacks stare,
And wonder if the thing is bull or bear!
Mad as a hornet, crazy as a bug,
He drags the bull Impeachment by the lug;
While "Kill the beast!" from every quarter's bawl'd,
Through ordure foul the battered brute is maul'd.
BUTLER rides him, and SUMNER goads him on,
While ELDRIDGE, happy wit, enjoys the fun.
The Cyclops form astride the wounded bull
Impedes his march, and makes his labor dull.
For food he pines, for food he must expire;
Close to his eyes in garbage, filth and mire,
Sweating and fuming, like the puffing Grote,
Huge ASHLEY thrusts an armful down his throat;
Cries—"O live, my bull! live my beauteous beast!
I know you're weak; but shake your tail, at least.
Many a kick, many a cuff and blow,
Since you were born, my pride (too true I know),
This robust form, this high aspiring head,
With meekness suffered, but in spirit bled;
My hopes, my life, my all on you depend;
Should you expire, poor ASHLEY's fame would end.
To rouse from coma, by all the gods (he swore),
Tonics I've sought from felon, pimp, and wh—e."

* Jeems saw some caricatures of himself leveling a gun at President
Johnson, while impeachment ruffians were suborning thieves and
felons, when he told a friend, in a very serious way, that he believed
he would be hereafter identified with the history of the country.

VIII.

The Speaker rises, and the hammer falls ;
The air is hush'd in silence round the walls.
All eyes are fixed on THAD, the mighty man,*
Who hawks, and talks, and spits where'er he can.
His puppets cluster round, draw close and near,
Proud to be spat upon by such a peer.
He boasts no topknot, but a wig, instead,
Imparts a grandeur to his awful head.
He spreads his broad bandanna, and he blows,
Then in some drowsy ear shoots half his nose ;
Affects a simper, and, with artless eyes,
Keeps in nice check a heart surcharged with lies.
Behold his palsied form, his shriveled trunk—
A wilted adder, by its venom shrunk.
However false—and better false than true,—
The leader's part must e'er be something new.
The puling truth is stale to every mind ;
While falsehood's ear is quick as falsehood's blind.
Weakness ! he cries, should a friend admonish ;
But, astonish ! death and hell, astonish !

* As these lines were written before the demise of this fanatical
theorist, we see no good reason for making any change. We do not
believe in that charity which forbears to speak of the course of a
public man after his death, when that course was one of living in
open adultery with a negro's wife for thirty odd years, and a sectional,
fanatical intolerance toward all political opponents.

IX.

When Nature slips, and makes some hideous thing,
The monster dies ere it can Nature sting.
When vile diseases seize the human form,
And woeful plagues around the being swarm,
And blood infectious clogs the coursing veins,
The wretch must die, from all his mortal pains.
STEVENS not so ; he lives a monster still,
Prepared to rob and plunder, starve and kill.
The kick, the cuff, by Indignation given ;
The lance of Scorn through every fiber driven ;
The fevered curses breathing for that life
Where Nature and the Devil are at strife,
Kill not the serpent ; still the reptile crawls,
And gluts upon the matter that he galls.

X.

Alas ! that bigots should be always blind !
Alas ! that man was born to scourge his kind !
Could not the piteous wail of infant years,
Of woman's prayers, or grief, or burning tears,
Upon his cheek bring one spontaneous glow
Of manhood's shame, or cause one tear to flow ?*

---

* A bill was introduced to the House of Representatives to appro-
priate some money for the purchase of food, to be given to starving
widows and orphans. Stevens and the Great American Spoon (Butler)

Whate'er the strife, howe'er the Fates may frown,
No soldier's arm would strike the vanquished down.
If there be man to show less generous part,
Then brand him "coward," with a tyrant's heart.
The narrow soul which on detraction feeds
Should know man's heart is better than his deeds.

    Let the base wretch, long bent with age and crime,
Forsake the streets his stealthy creepings slime;
Crawl to some dungeon, far from human sight,
That, like his own heart, is as black as night,
And where the worms, sprung from the nauseous dead,
May on his carcass lustily be fed.
Hence let him go, to find at last his place,
Loathed by the good, and hated by his race!

XI.

    The play begins, and BOUTWELL is the clown.
THAD drops the simper, and assumes a frown.
"Now thousand tongues are heard in one loud din;
The monkey mimics rush discordant in;"
And fawning BOYNTON shakes his ourang head,
And echoes bigots for his menial bread.

---

opposed the appropriation with their accustomed bitterness and sectionalism. It was stated in advocacy of the bill, that sixteen children, whose ages were from two to ten years, being at the point of starvation, were collected round a Southern man's table, and given a meal—the first some of them had eaten in twenty-four hours. Stevens' response to this was: "Let them starve - they are children of rebels!"

Let BOUTWELL snivel, and let LOGAN yell,
Send unbelievers in their cant to hell ;
While SCHENCK, the mighty warrior, strikes his blows,
With finger pointed at the Speaker's nose,
And spurts, and blurts, and jumps like any cub,
And pumps himself of froth, plup-plup, and blub.
They're dextrous, agile circus-riders all,
And lash the steed of Progress round the hall.
The Constitution forms the paper ring
Through which the frisky jugglers skip and spring :
And round and round the wildest furies run,
Till blacks seem angels, radiant as the sun,
And heinous rebels, frightful serpents, fall
Upon the steed, and turn him into gall ;
And as his quivering limbs still urge the flight,
The steed sees BUTLER, and expires of fright ;
While rival monkeys, wounded in the race,
Go whining round, and smut each other's face,
And swell with wrath, as choler rages high,
And glance across their nose with glazed eye.

XII.

Lo! now my BUTLER, with a head of brass,
Outroars the " clarion of the braying ass!"
Callous and hide-bound to both good and ill,
No scorn can wound the fool, nor scoffing kill.
" Double the guard !" the livelong day he cries ;
In sleep, nice spoons appear before his eyes.

See the great grampus! Lord, how strong he blows,
As waspish BINGHAM strokes and tweags his nose!*
He snorts, he bawls, the wildest of buffoons,
And swears those urchins lie who call him "Spoons."

XIII.

How long shall prate usurp the laws of sense,
And graceless creatures stand on sheer pretense?
Will men not read the future of their fate?
Can men not see that Congress saps the State?
Here pimps get office through their favored bawds,
And harlots lobby for nefarious frauds;
In ante-rooms display their bosoms bare,
And name the price, and seal agreement there.

XIV.

Heavens! my head! What caused the air to crack?
I see, I see. Alas, 'tis dirty Jack.†

---

* The tilt between the Falstaffian Butler and the vinegar-faced
Bingham, on the floor of the House, was one of the most amusing
things of the Fortieth Congress. Bingham accused Butler of living
in a bottle and being fed with a spoon; when Butler retaliated by
accusing Bingham of hanging an innocent woman (Mrs. Surratt).

† John Covode, known as "Dirty Jack." He is the sport and butt
of the House. He claims to represent the "sheep" interest of Penn-
sylvania. No member will sit near him on account of his dirty
habits.

Pity the foe whom dirty Jack assails,
With filthy speech, and with more filthy nails.
His arms, like handspikes, the wide circle sweep,
Strikes his bold breast, as echo answers, " Sheep!" .

XV.

'Tis the night when all the monkeys muster,
To smoke and drink, swear, and fillibuster.
There's whisking, frisking, nodding, plodding round,
And looks that warn the weak to stand their ground.
To fetichism the monkeys gravely nod,
And scout the laws of Nature and her God.

XVI.

Calm SCHUYLER views the medley from his throne,
And quells the murmurs of the buzzing drone;
And 'midst the twanging of a thousand tongues,
Explains, decides, corrects, and wastes his lungs.
With ponderous sound the Stentor calls the roll,
Whose tymbal mouthings jar the tender soul.
But frisky monkeys are, like men, but clay;
Salacious pleasures some have forced away.
He's gone! he's gone! In vain the Stentor calls!

Dispatch the herald! make search at MARY HALL'S!*
There, in ambrosia,† melt odahlic charms,
Involving Love 'twixt generous legs and arms.
The Sergeant knocks; the "battered jades" appear:
"It is—ah, no!—oh, yes!—walk in, my dear!"
Timid at first, then marching with a stride,
He chides his courage, and he pricks his pride.
With pompous mien, and cold official gaze,
Around he stalks, and marvels at his ways.
To meet his glance the punks are coyly shy,
While mirrors praise the sternness of his eye.
He gazed, and gazed, and gazing lost his thought;
When reverie supplied the thing he sought.
He rummaged, searched, till he was nearly blind,
Which somewhat ruffled his official mind.
Yielding, at last, to rashness and despair,
He kicked a couch, and what d'ye think found there?
I leave the theme, and leave for you to guess
The looks of mental horror and distress.
The rumor goes that HARPER'S fool was there,
And etched the scene, ensconced beneath a chair.
By times, 'tis said, he wings him to the moon,
To sketch the straining ship in a typhoon.

* It is a most scandalous fact, that during the evening sessions of
Congress, when the Sergeant-at-Arms is directed to hunt up delin-
quent members, the first place he searches for them is this notorious
house of prostitution.

† Ambrosia, love reciprocated. *Language of Flowers.*

XVII.

From monkey mimics, owls and bats I fly!
Who stays my pen? Ye fiends and furies—NYE!
Prodigious NYE! antic, wit, and jester!
Pride of the Stump, and of Cant the Nestor!
Now drop your heads, ye gentle creatures, low,
And calmly hear the Western Slasher blow!
With sudden bounce he sallies on the floor,
While wondering eyes survey the horrid boor.
Like the poor wretch, long starving for his bread,
When some good luck of fortune turns his head,
NYE laughs, then weeps, then glares with fool's surprise;
Now jumps and roars, now laughs again, now sighs;
For all is vast and "mighty" in his eyes.*

XVIII.

Now there reclines at ease McCULLOCH'S foe;
A mawkish, tawdry fop from top to toe;
The pride of Boston, or, as some would dub
That codfish port, New Athens or the Hub;
Big with great hope, proud thoughts, and vanity,
Soaring on nonsense and inanity.

---

* "This mighty Congress; this mighty nation; this mighty people;
our mighty and stupendous army; our mighty and prodigious navy."
—Nye's speeches in the Senate.

Pedantic SUMNER! full of heavy books,*
Which he affects to tell you in his looks.
He twiddles, piddles, smooths and pets his locks;
To this he's deaf, to that his ear he cocks.
With lords and dukes the glib-tongued SUMNER dined,
Hobnobbed with knights, and flunkied to their kind;
He guzzled negus with a seedy count,
And caught the itch of snobbery at its fount.
When he yawns, 'tis as my lord De Assy;
When he mouths, 'tis as the count de Gassy.
He wears a gegaw; toys with it as naught;
Then pinches it severely for a thought.
In silent glances and a deep profound,
His meditations cast their shadows round.
He shakes his locks; he has a little bill,†
(The stuff, to-morrow, half the *Globe* will fill;)
And here's a missive from an honest friend—
(Pish! pah! ye gods, where will this twaddle end?)
Those wicked rebels (men, forbear to sleep,)
Still cuff the negro, and decline to weep.
He prates and mouths, and mouths and prates again,
Till all feign sleep, but sleep and snore in vain.

    "God grant me patience!" thus a member said;

---

* "The bookful blockhead, ignorantly read,
    With loads of learned lumber in his head."

† Sumner occupies, almost daily, the time of the Senate in reading letters from Southern Carpet-baggers and Scalawags, bitterly complaining that the Southern people are suffered to live, and beseeching Congress to give the petitioners control of all the plantations.

And rubbed his eyes, and dropp'd again his head.

" O Lord, how long?" another member cried,

Then stretched and yawned, and stamp'd his feet, and
      sighed ;

And weary looks displayed some little spleen,

And wondered what the devil he could mean.

As some bold knave, well practised in a fraud,

Devises tricks for dunces to applaud,

His plots and plans must ne'er be understood ;

They're far too lofty for the low and rude.

    With spirit sad he drops his heavy head,

And thinks of all his mourners when he's dead :

The beauty of his hands they'll eulogize,

And praise his figure and his stately size ;*

How much h. shaved, how long his whiskers grew,

And that his nose was Roman—not a Jew ;

All this, and more, they'll know, as long they knew.

He dreams of paintings—what time 'twill require

To daub and brush, and lend his visage fire ;

For some Raphael he's moved with tender sighs.

For who can give expression to his eyes ?

Now, on the wing of fame he proudly soars,

As, rapt in his sweet self, he smiles and pours

O'er the smooth diction of his classic mind,†

Sententious, trenchant, charmingly refined.

---

* "For stateliness and majesty, what is comparable to a Horse?"--*More.*

† "Next o'er his books his eyes began to roll,
    In pleasing memory of all he stole."

In subtle phrase he's doomed to atticise,
And fill the Senate with the gravest lies.*

XIX.

What sound so jars upon my wounded ear?
A donkey brays—a WILSON doth appear.
The Natic cobbler flings aside his awl,
Pricks his long ears as other donkeys bawl;
His eyes dilate; he stands in steady gaze,
While all his brothers scan his wondrous ways.
His ears are spread; his neck far reaches o'er
The heads and tails of many donkeys more.
    "A question grave doth stick to me like wax,"
The cobbler cries. "Suppose we all were blacks,
And there was no sun, and the moon were blue,
Then what would donkeys and the cobblers do?"
    With steering tails wild o'er the green they play
"Bravo! bravo!" round all the donkeys bray.
"Raise me aloft! Keep stiff each friendly tail!
While wax is wax let no weak donkey quail.
Raise me aloft! and when I'm o'er the bars,
Behold a WEBSTER!‡ thank your loyal stars!"
No honest donkey could at this demur,

---

* "Destroy his fib, or sophistry, in vain!
        The creature's at his dirty work again."

  † This sputtering creature once boasted he FILLED Daniel Webster's
seat in the Senate. Shades of Webster!

Though there were barks from some dissenting cur.
He whisked his tail; he snuffed the balmy breeze;
The bars were reached; the mount was made with ease.
Now perched aloft upon the giddy height,
The frisky cobbler brayed with all his might;
And winds and tides, and earth, and sky, and air
Were hushed, or shaken with awful noise and blare.
O'er mazing herds he spread a dizzy pall;
'Twas muddle, muddle, and dumfuddle all.
Some wept, some prayed, some wished they ne'er were
 born;
It must be Satan or Saint Gabriel's horn.
Yet hark again! What means that merry roar?
Guffaws reply—"It is the Natick bore."

 In all the casts of hugeness not to fail,
O'er slops and pots of gravy, punch, and ale,
He shook his checks, he shook his head and eyes,
Till paunch and stomach found relief in sighs.
The clang, the bang, the awful sound of war,
The waking trumpet, rousing from afar,
Lent martial music to the cobbler's soul;
Nor wax, nor tax could stay him nor control.
Away! away! His blood ran fierce and wild!
A thousand foemen with one stroke he pil'd!
A thousand more, before yon sun is set,
Shall sink beneath his blade, all dripping wet!

XX.

Along the streets, with calm equestrian grace,
On piebald nag proud WILSON squares his face.
The ladies smile, and all admire his rank,
As keenly prick his spurs the piebald's flank.
O'er all the scope of history's gory page
He felt the hero, and he looked the sage.
He thought of sabers brandished high in air,
Of roaring cannon and the trumpet's blare,
And routed armies, fleeing in despair,
And groaning chieftains by their mangled steeds,
New Marathons, and other Spartan deeds;
How yonder phalanx shows a deadly breach,
As through its ranks the shells from cannon screech;
And where the sward is slippery with the slain,
The surging columns meet and press amain.
On every spear there lives a poisoned breath,
And plunging life doth yield a quivering death;
And troopers wild, with roar and headlong speed,
Sharing the will of their proud mettled steed;
Quick, quick, and on, where high the chargers neigh,
With lightning dash they madly join the fray.
A thousand steeds at equal numbers run;
Two thousand swords flash crescents in the sun;
And men there fight as men ne'er fought before;
And heroes fall who'll ne'er be mentioned more.
All this he viewed with calm, prophetic eye;
And then he thought of death, and heaved a sigh.

He hailed his henchman, and he ordered wine ;
Then doffed his spurs, and swore he would resign.

Alas, the shame!   In Congress bigots prate,
And blind fanatics rule the ruined State ;
High on the rostrum wild viragos screech ;
The pulpit mount, and to their cuckolds preach.
See the bold spinster, spurned and cast aside,
Proclaim the wants she can no longer hide !
In tender years, when that blanch'd face was fair,
And flowing ringlets woo'd the gentle air ;
When modest sweetness on that brow was traced,
And all the graces all her movements graced ;
That clear blue eye of innocence and youth,
At once the mirror and the soul of truth,
Appeared, like Venus in the Vesper blue,
When toil finds rest and hope is born anew ;
Who then would dream that, ere her life was o'er,
Discarding sex—alas ! discarding more !—
Temples and fanes would ring with her harangue,
And things called men indulge her flippant slang ?

ANNIE, (sweet, gentle ANNIE of the Vale,
I mean not thee, but ANNIE old and stale,)
How fare stump speeches and their needful boons ?

How fares each audience of poor, spoony loons,
Who hark complacent to your foolish cant,
And loudly echo all your silly rant?
See the vile batch of shameless, toothless dames,
Whose voice I dread more than Erebus' flames,
Intrude their faces, daub'd with paint and glue,
Which fill their wrinkles, make their blushes new;
Deck'd with long tufts, which dare to strife the gale,
Pluck'd from a corse, or some poor horse's tail;
These tufts adorning, scarlet streamers bind,
Which whip and wriggle to their waists behind.
Their mouths they ope, which seem like tombless graves,
Through which the wind in moaning sadness raves.
These horrid hags their doleful pates extend;
Dilate on wedlock—how each race should blend!
What nuptial bliss blest Hymen will bestow,
If we but practise secrets which they know!
Were social forms and social customs rent,
The pining spinster ne'er would sneeze at scent!
Her hopes declining with her ebbing charms,
Would greet with joy black Sambo's unctuous arms!
O! shades of Hades! how my soul detests
These rueful wrecks of Nature's proud behests!
Depraved, presumptuous, to all reason blind,
They are a living lie on womankind!

  The mouldering hag becomes a cooing dove,
Proclaims affinity, and asserts her love!
Should unbelievers know the reason why,
The table raps a quick and prompt reply.
Since burning witches claim no more the stage,

Spirits of air the driv'ling fools engage ;
And Cotton Mather soars aloft again,
Dispatched from hell, with all his motley train.

XXIII.

Conscience—mercurial bird of Freedom's birth,
Whose bars and confines ne'er were made for earth ;
Whose love of Right illumes the human clay,
And gilds with Hope the brightness of its day ;
Holds forth the goal of rest beyond the stars,
And flaps with joyous wings its prison bars;
Then sings of Freedom in its mundane cell,
Till seraph voices with its music swell,
Rising harmonic with the heavenly soul,
When bliss eternal's reach'd in its control :
Spirit of Williams!* well thou couldst attest
How conscience suffered in the freeman's breast,
When blind fanatics, in religion's name,
Prepared the fagot, and raised high the flame.

XXIV.

I'll hie to church ! With Beecher's lambs I'll pray,
And laugh, good-natured, at the merry play.

---

* Roger Williams, who, for freedom of conscience, had to flee from
the wrath of the Puritan bigots.

The deacon moves before the saintly door,
Bows in the wealthy, and bows out the poor;
Down long, broad aisles pass saints of every mold :
The ogling, jealous, and the saints who scold;
The merchant saints, whose diamonds shine afar,
On fingers cleanly scrubbed of pitch and tar;
The premium saint, whose pew we closely scan,
As round the whisper goes that "he's the man!"
.The saint who grunts, and with a solid launch,
Down bears his seat, and forth distends his paunch,
Wipes from his brow some drops of heavy dew,
Then puffs and swells, as barley malt doth brew;
The saint of musk, whose kerchief scents the air :
The hoary saint, who dyes his grizzly hair;
The painted saint, with curls to order made;
The saint of hat and plume, and rich brocade;
The false-toothed saint, who would a prayer beguile
To take observance, and to yield a smile;
The saint who giveth, as the plate goes round,
To Heaven a gift of which he robb'd the town.
Adown the vistas of this motley throng
The eye's bewildered as it shoots along;
The eye is pleased to view the fairy dell;
The mind revolts at the alluring hell.

XXV.

At length from dreadful screams the stranger's freed.
Be quiet all! The show will soon proceed.

On yon plump form, adorned with yellow hair,
All eyes are fixed with most punctilious care.
With startled look he makes a quick survey
Of all the asses who came there to bray.
As o'er his chest his arms conversely slip,
A studied gesture waits upon his lip.
He bends, he shakes ; a word, a toss, a bow.
Wild beasts, be still !   There's storm on BEECHER's brow !
His theme is Sambo, and demands his rage,
Like Vengeance strutting on the mimic stage.
Ope wide your mouths, and let his rant go down,
In sighs returning for the martyred BROWN !
He kicks, he stamps ; he lashes to and fro,
And, with his cant, at reason strikes a blow ;
Back casts his hair, like Sappho ere the plunge,
And makes at mouths agape a forward lunge.
He fumes, he foams—drowns sense with every shout,
Like thought bewildered in a tipsy rout.
With tricks like these the parson earns his prog,
While some cry " Shame !" and others, " Demagogue !"

XXVI.

RAYMOND, come forth ! or JENKINS, as they call,
Since you donn'd breeches for a Paris ball.
They must have laughed (the Lolas and the Peggs),
As round you capered with your bandy legs,
And patted you, and gave you sugar plum,
And whispered, " Lord ! is this the pigmy THUMB ?"

You are the trimmer—so your HORACE says ;
And he accords you all your meed of praise.
He called you " villain" once—a cut unkind—
Which shows ill temper sometimes sways his mind.
But then, my dapper youth, be of good cheer ;
Trim well your sails, and watch the winds that veer.
Connive, betray, assert, and then deny ;
Long panting fame will soar upon a lie.

XXVII.

Who e'er, ye gods, who e'er saw GREELEY's feet,
Spavined and halt, lumbering through the street?
His knees, like puppets in a penny show,
Fight as they pass, and crack at each a blow.
His thoughts to give a more abstracted air,
The pants fall short, and half the shanks are bare.
His bunion boots are large and strangely rude,
Through some blest holes of which his kibes protrude.
Along the street with jerk and halt he struts,
Munching wild grapes or gobbling hickory nuts.
Soft seems his heart with gentle, humane sighs,
When foes are sped, or an enemy dies ;
But Oh, the poison of his railing tongue
When he is crossed, or his great heart is wrung.
A native rustic and a would-be wit,
He dons his garments, careless of their fit,
O'er which he slavers with a thoughtless spit.

XXVIII.

Now, you weak creatures, you who hold the power,
(The pleasing bubble of the passing hour,)
Behind the murdered murder still to cause,
To gain the bigot's or the fool's applause,
At once give o'er; abate your ruffian howl,
And THAD's sereneness mock Minerva's owl.

XXIX.

The wild for fame the shame of guilt will woo,
And take from outlaws their successful cue.
As men are hush'd in awe, surprise, or fear,
When crimes inhuman pall upon the ear,
The moral sense to shock the trickster tries,
And courts abuse if he to notice rise.

XXX.

While mine the part to elevate the slave,
Encourage worth, applaud the true and brave,
I would not weigh my gold against the sand,
Nor trust my weal to the unlettered hand.
Let Virtue, Knowledge, Honor, rule the State,
And Wisdom guard, and Truth direct her fate;
As Truth, Time's handmaid, must forever roll,
In long, deep whispers, through the godlike soul.

www.ingramcontent.com/pod-product-compliance
Lightning Source LLC
Chambersburg PA
CBHW030915260626

47169CB00008B/2864